P9-EMQ-996

The Next Karate Kid

A novel by B.B. Hiller
From a screenplay written by Mark Lee
Based on characters created by Robert Mark Kamen

SCHOLASTIC INC.
New York Toronto London Auckland Sydney

The Next Karate Kid

COLUMBIA PICTURES PRESENTS

A JERRY WEINTRAUB PRODUCTION A FILM BY CHRISTOPHER CAIN STARRING NORIYUKI "PAT" MORITA HILARY SWANK
"THE NEXT KARATE KID" MICHAEL IRONSIDE MUSIC BY BILL CONTI
EXECUTIVE PRODUCER R.J. LOUIS WRITTEN BY MARK LEE PRODUCED BY JERRY WEINTRAUB DIRECTED BY CHRISTOPHER CAIN

COLUMBIA
PICTURES

© 1994 Columbia Pictures Industries, Inc. All rights reserved.

For Andy

If you purchased this book without a cover, you should be aware that this book is stolen property. It was reported as "unsold and destroyed" to the publisher, and neither the author nor the publisher has received any payment for this "stripped book."

No part of this publication may be reproduced in whole or in part, or stored in a retrieval system, or transmitted in any form or by any means, electronic, mechanical, photocopying, recording, or otherwise, without written permission of the publisher. For information regarding permission, write to Scholastic Inc., 555 Broadway, New York, NY 10012.

ISBN 0-590-48445-1

Copyright © 1994 Columbia Pictures Industries, Inc. All rights reserved.
Published by Scholastic Inc.

12 11 10 9 8 7 6 5 4 3 2   4 5 6 7 8 9/9

Printed in the U.S.A.   40

First Scholastic printing, July 1994

1

Julie Pierce was angry all the time. She was angry at her teachers. She was angry at her classmates. She was angry at her grandmother. Most of all, she was angry at her parents for dying in a car accident. Nothing had seemed to go right since that happened and she'd moved in with Grandma.

She didn't trust anybody, either. The only creature in the world she could talk to was Angel. Angel was a hawk with a broken wing. Julie had found Angel near her high school. She was sure if anybody knew about Angel, they would take her away, so she hid her in an old pigeon coop on the roof of the school. She fed her fresh meat and gave her water and talked to her. She could tell Angel anything.

One day, she had not been able to get food to Angel during the daytime, so she had to go at night. She'd taken some hamburger from her grandmother's refrigerator and she snuck over to the school. She knew a secret way to get in through one of the classrooms. It only took her a minute to get to the roof, but while she walked up the stairs, she thought about the man who was at Grandma's house.

He was an old man, almost as old as Grandma. Grandma said something about the fact that he had been in the army with Grandpa during World War II. He looked old enough for that! His name was Mr. Miyagi.

Grandpa had been a brave officer. He'd even gotten the Congressional Medal of Honor. That was the highest honor an American serviceman could get. But that was a long time ago. Julie didn't care what had happened a long time ago. She only cared about feeding Angel.

Finally, she opened the last door and was on the roof. Angel seemed to be waiting for her. Julie put a long leather glove on her left hand and reached into the cage. Angel hopped onto Julie's wrist. She had sharp claws called talons that might scratch Julie without the glove. Julie knew Angel would never try to hurt her. She just couldn't help herself.

"How's your wing, Angel?" she asked. The bird flapped her wings a little. Her left wing hung oddly. It was still broken, but Julie was sure it was getting better.

Julie gave Angel the meat and talked to her as she ate. "I got into another argument with

Grandma tonight. She wanted me to meet this old guy, but I had to get here to feed you. I don't know why she can't just leave me alone. I wish everybody would leave me alone!"

Angel gulped and asked for more food. Julie gave her the last of the hamburger. She talked some more. "If they found out you were here, they'd take you away. Isn't that awful?"

Angel cocked her head to the right. Julie was sure that was a "yes."

When Angel finished eating, Julie stood up and walked around the roof. Angel was still sitting on her wrist, but she wasn't going to fly away.

It was a beautiful night. There was a full moon and just a few clouds. Being on top of the school was almost like flying. Julie spread her arms out, pretending she could fly just as Angel would be able to do one of these days.

"I wish we could just fly away together," she said. "Wouldn't that be great? We'd never have arguments and you'd never tell me what to do. We'd fly up through the clouds and . . ."

Julie heard a car door slam below. She looked over the edge of the roof. There was a police car right in front of the school and she realized the policemen must have seen her. She didn't care if they caught her, but she did care if they found Angel. She didn't have a second to spare.

She ran back to Angel's cage and put the hawk inside for the night. She locked the cage and then she hid behind it. When the policemen got to the roof, Julie threw her flashlight at them. It surprised them and that gave Julie the chance she needed to run. She ran as fast as she ever had and the police followed her. Julie was much faster than the policemen and that was good news. Even better was the fact that as long as they followed her, they'd never find Angel.

Julie was down the stairs and out the door long before the policemen got to the ground floor. By the time she'd gone a block from the school, she knew she was safe — for now.

2

When Julie got home, she had a surprise. Her grandmother had decided to go to California and stay in Mr. Miyagi's house for a while. Mr. Miyagi was going to stay in Grandma's house with Julie.

"I love you, Julie. And I know that you love me, but these days we act like we hate each other. Maybe we just each need some time apart."

"But Grandma . . ."

"Mr. Miyagi's a good man, a wise man. I don't know if he can help us, but at least we won't be yelling at each other all the time."

Julie didn't know what to think. These days, everything confused her. It was usually easier *not* to think. She decided to do that. What difference did it make who stayed with her?

She rode with Mr. Miyagi when he took Grandma to the airport and then he drove her to school. Mr. Miyagi tried to pretend it was okay.

"Grandmother miss you already," he said.

"I doubt that," Julie told him. "My birthday's in a couple of weeks. Guess she forgot."

"A birthday very special day. Miyagi will cook special Japanese dinner for you. Tempura? Sukiyaki? You like?"

Grandma always made tacos for Julie on her birthday, but if Grandma didn't care enough to be there for it, then Julie wouldn't care what she ate. "I don't need a dinner," she said. "I can take care of myself. I know where I'm going."

"*Hai*," said Mr. Miyagi. It was the Japanese word for "yes." Mr. Miyagi said it a lot. "Miyagi also know where you're going. Going to school." He drove up in front of the high school. "Pick you up here this afternoon. Okay? Julie?"

Julie got out of the car. It looked as if Mr. Miyagi wasn't just planning to stay with her, but he was also going to baby-sit her. She could get home by herself. She just slammed the car door and walked into the school. She didn't even say goodbye.

The first thing she saw inside was the first thing she saw every morning. It was a group of students called the Alpha Elite. Their leader was a man named Col. Dugan. Col. Dugan was in charge of the Alphas and the Alphas were in charge of "security" during the school day. As near as Julie could tell, that meant they had a license to be bullies.

6

When the first bell rang, the students had three minutes to get to class. The Alphas started their "sweep" of the halls, hurrying the students along. The students were afraid of the Alphas. They did what they were told.

Julie hurried along, but she didn't hurry to class. She hurried to her hiding place. She didn't want to go to science. She wanted to be by herself. Her hiding place was an old greenhouse that wasn't being used. She lay down on a pillow and put on her earphones. She clicked some buttons on her tape player and listened to Prince. He was her favorite.

She closed her eyes and listened to the music. She could feel the warm sunshine that came streaming through the panes of glass in the greenhouse. It was much nicer than science. Then something blocked her sunlight. She opened her eyes. Ned Randall was standing there.

Ned was one of the Alphas. As far as Julie was concerned, he was the worst of them, too. He was the biggest bully of the bunch. He also had the idea that the girls — especially Julie — all thought he was cool. Julie didn't know what the other girls thought, but she wasn't interested.

"You could be in big trouble here, Julie," Ned said.

"Drop dead," she suggested.

"I *could* take you to the principal's office, or you could go out with me tomorrow night."

"No way."

"Julie, if you start going out with me, you'll be able to get away with anything you want in this school. The Alphas run the place. You know that."

She did know that, but it didn't tempt her to go on a date with Ned Randall.

"I don't want any part of you or your Alphas," she said.

He was angry that she turned him down. He grabbed her by the wrist. She was a little afraid of what he might do, but Col. Dugan arrived just in time.

"What's goin' on, Ned?"

Then Ned lied. He told Col. Dugan that Julie had been smoking, and Col. Dugan took her right to the principal's office.

The principal, Mr. Wilkes, took Col. Dugan's word without even asking Julie if it were true. Julie was upset, but it was about what she expected from Ned, from the Alphas, from the principal, and from the whole world. She didn't care, either.

"This is a serious matter, Julie. You could have accidentally started a fire and burned down the school."

"No big loss," she said. That was the way she felt, too.

Col. Dugan made Mr. Wilkes promise that if Julie broke another rule — no matter what — he'd suspend her. Mr. Wilkes seemed willing to do anything Col. Dugan said. Julie thought Col. Dugan was a bigger bully than Ned Randall. He even bullied the principal.

Col. Dugan told one of the Alphas to take Julie to her next class. He didn't look like the other Alphas to Julie. He had a nice smile and a friendly manner. But anybody who was a friend of Col. Dugan's was no friend of hers.

"I'm Eric McGowen. What's your name?" he said.

"Don't try to be nice," she answered. "You're just another one of Dugan's jerks."

Eric was surprised by what she said. He told her that he was new in the school, but at his old school, everybody talked about the Alphas. "It's famous, like a championship football team," he said. "I really wanted to be here to be a part of it even though Col. Dugan can be a little tough sometimes."

Tough wasn't the word Julie would have used. She didn't see any point in discussing it with Eric, though. She just wanted to get away from him. She stopped in front of the girls' room and went in. He'd never follow her there and he'd never catch her, either.

This girls' room had a window to the fire escape. The fire escape went up to the roof. Julie decided to visit Angel. She wondered how long Eric would stand outside the girls' room door. That made her laugh for the first time that day.

3

Angel was just fine. She seemed happy to see Julie and she seemed especially happy to have the food Julie brought.

"How's the wing?" Julie asked. "Does it feel any better? Don't worry, Angel. I'm not going to leave you."

Julie heard a noise behind her. It was the gate opening. She turned around. There was Eric!

"There's a Keep Out sign. Can't you read?"

Eric didn't answer her question. Instead, he asked one of his own. "Where'd you get the hawk?"

"I found it in the grass near the gym," she said.

"Does it bite?"

Angel screeched. "Yes," Julie said. "So stay back."

Eric stayed back. He seemed like a nice enough boy, but he *was* an Alpha, and now he knew about Angel. She was going to have to find a way to get him to keep her secret. She didn't like that idea.

"This is my secret. All right?"

"It *was* your secret."

He seemed to be teasing a little in a nice way, but Julie couldn't be sure. She had to be sure. She put Angel back in the cage and the two of them went back to school. As they walked down the stairs, Julie tried again to make Eric promise not to tell.

"You tell anybody about this and you're going to be in trouble."

"Really? What kind of trouble?"

Julie thought for a second. She had an idea. "I'll call the pizza shop and have them deliver forty-eight pizzas to your house at one o'clock in the morning."

"No anchovies, okay?"

Then they were in a hallway and the bell rang. It was time for their next class. Eric stepped into his classroom. Julie wasn't going to get an answer from him — at least not then. She went to her next class and decided she'd figure out what to do later.

The next time Julie saw Eric, he didn't see her. They didn't have any classes together, but she knew he would be at his Alpha practice that afternoon. Julie had always wanted to know exactly *what* the Alphas practiced and now she would find out. Col. Dugan was very secretive about their practices. They took place at the far end of the athletic field, behind the football bleachers. He never let anybody watch. But that didn't stop Julie. She hid under the bleachers, behind a stack of folding chairs. She could see them and they couldn't see her. She'd wait until she had a chance to talk to Eric. And if she couldn't talk to him at practice, she'd follow him until she could talk to him.

Col. Dugan called everybody to attention. The Alphas stood in a straight line. Col. Dugan gave a scary speech about enemies. Julie didn't know who he was talking about. Then he said, "Now, the enemies are *inside* our country, inside our cities, inside our *schools!*"

Eric leaned over to Ned and whispered, "What enemies?" That was the same question Julie would have asked.

"Shut up," said Ned.

Dugan began the physical exercise then. The Alphas made a circle around him and he told them they should try to attack him. They tried, one at a time. And one at a time, he beat them. He didn't just pin them. He punched them and kicked them. Some of them were really hurt. Julie thought that was crazy.

Eric thought it was crazy, too. He refused to fight Col. Dugan.

"Look, I'll fight for myself or my family, but I won't fight just to prove how tough you are."

Col. Dugan slapped him in the face. That made Eric angry. He tried to punch the colonel, but he didn't hit him. Col. Dugan blocked the punch and then he smiled. "There you go," he said. "That's what I want to see. Get angry!"

Eric attacked hard then, but the colonel was too good for him. It only took a minute for Col. Dugan to beat Eric. Eric was on the ground and his nose was bleeding. Julie wanted to run out to him, but she knew she couldn't. She was trying to figure out if there was some way she could stop the fight when someone else did it for her: Mr. Miyagi!

She hadn't seen him coming, but there he was, and he was looking for her!

Col. Dugan told him to go away. Mr. Miyagi didn't go away, though, he went over to Eric.

"You all right?" he asked.

"No problem," Eric said. He stood up. Julie could see he *was* all right — barely.

Col. Dugan didn't like having Mr. Miyagi there. "I told you to get out of here. Are you deaf?"

"Hearing okay," said Mr. Miyagi.

"Then something must be wrong with your brain because I told you to leave and you're still here!"

Mr. Miyagi didn't seem at all upset. He remained polite as he spoke to Col. Dugan. "Miyagi grew up in village on Okinawa. Bad-tempered bull lived in pasture near village. Bull chased children. Chased market women. Chased farmer, too — until big festival."

13

Julie could tell that Col. Dugan really wanted Mr. Miyagi to leave, but even more, he wanted to know what Mr. Miyagi was talking about.

"What are you saying? What happened to the bull at the festival?"

"That day bad bull became good soup."

Col. Dugan was furious. Julie wanted to laugh. She had a mental picture of Col. Dugan in a big black pot — becoming good soup!

4

Julie found Eric by his car after Alpha practice. He was surprised to see her.

"Did you tell Dugan about the hawk?" she asked.

"You stayed after school to ask me that?"

"If anybody finds out about Angel, they're going to take her away."

Eric got into his car. Julie climbed in on the passenger side. She just couldn't let him leave her there without telling her.

He started the engine. She didn't move.

"I'm going to work," he said.

She didn't move. He didn't answer her question. He just drove.

Twenty minutes later, Eric drove his car into a train yard. It was a sort of open garage for passenger and freight cars that weren't being used. He got out of the car and put on a cap and a shirt.

"You're a security guard?" Julie asked.

"You got it. I work the night shift."

He walked around the yard to check that everything was in order.

"My grandfather was an engineer at this train yard," he explained. Julie could tell he was proud of his grandfather.

Eric climbed onto the top of a car and then he helped Julie up as well. It was nice to stand up there. Julie could see for miles. There were a lot of trains, but there was also the big city of Boston beyond them and then, to the west, the sun was setting. It was very pretty.

"Why do you do this?" Julie asked.

"For the money," he said. "My dad left my mother a while ago and there's never enough money. But this job is only temporary. I'm going to the Air Force Academy and learn how to be a pilot. Col. Dugan said he can get me in."

That explained why somebody who seemed to be a fairly nice human being would hang around with the Alphas. It also meant that maybe, just maybe, Eric wouldn't tell about Angel.

"I'm going to make you promise me that you won't tell anybody about the hawk," she said.

"Don't worry."

"Promise."

"If it's really that important . . ."

"*Promise.*"

"Okay. I promise."

Julie sighed with relief. Angel was safe. That was all she cared about.

5

When Julie got back from the train yard, she tried to sneak into the house. She knew Mr. Miyagi would be upset that she wasn't there after school and she didn't want to get a lecture.

Mr. Miyagi was waiting for her when she arrived. She couldn't sneak past him.

"Miyagi go to school this afternoon. Look for Julie-san. You not there."

It sounded funny to Julie when he called her "Julie-san," but she knew that in his homeland, adding "san" after someone's name was a sign of respect. In spite of the respect, she knew there was more to come. She waited.

"Miyagi also talk to people — your teachers. Got homework you've missed for the last three weeks."

"Great. Maybe I'll do it sometime."

"Maybe do it tonight."

"Don't order me around!"

"It is request, Julie-san."

It didn't sound like a request to Julie. It just made her angry. She didn't want to listen anymore. She ran out of the house. She ran across the yard, over the sidewalk, and into the street. She didn't know where she was running. She was just running away.

She was in such a hurry that she didn't see the car careening around the corner. She only saw it when its brakes started screeching and then it was too late. It was going to hit her!

Julie did the only thing she could think of. She jumped right onto the hood of the car. The car came to a halt and Julie landed. She landed with one foot in front of the other, evenly balanced between them. She also had one hand up as if to block a high punch and the other waist high, ready to attack.

Mr. Miyagi arrived then. He helped her down off the car.

"Are you hurt, Julie-san?" he asked.

"I'm okay," she said.

He took her into the house and they sat down in the parlor. Julie had been frightened. She was shaking and she was angry, too.

"Go ahead. Do what my grandmother does. Tell me I made another mistake. 'Julie, you're so thoughtless!' and 'Julie, you lost your temper again!' "

"No need for Miyagi to speak. You do very good job. Thank you," he said.

Julie was finding him totally unpredictable and that annoyed her in a way she couldn't describe.

"Aren't you going to say anything?"

"Where did you learn that?"

"Learn what?"

"You leap into karate position when car threatens you. Not something they teach in girls' gym."

She hadn't thought about it, but it was true. She looked over at the piano where Grandma kept the family pictures. Mr. Miyagi looked where she looked. He saw a picture of Julie and her father when she was about eight. They were each wearing a karate outfit, called a *gi*. She'd almost forgotten.

"My father taught me karate when I was a little girl. We used to do it every night after school. I thought it was a game."

Mr. Miyagi nodded. "*Hai*. Julie-san's grandfather save Miyagi's life in battle so Miyagi teach him karate. He teach your father, so father teach you."

It made Julie remember and remembering made her feel angry again. "Then they died. Everybody died."

"Anger not bring them back, Julie-san."

Julie looked at all the pictures. Sometimes it was hard for her to remember her parents. Looking at the pictures didn't always help.

Mr. Miyagi seemed to understand that. "Parents leave more than photographs, Julie-san. They leave memories, knowledge, karate."

"What's so special about that?"

Mr. Miyagi touched his heart. "Real karate is *here* Julie-san. At time, you were too young to learn real lesson."

Julie was frustrated. "For once, I'd like you to give me an answer I can understand!"

"Answer not important if ask right question," said Mr. Miyagi.

"That's exactly what I'm talking about!" she shouted. Then she ran upstairs.

Julie thought all night long about what Mr. Miyagi had said. When morning came, she thought she knew what the right question was and she asked it.

"Mr. Miyagi, could you teach me karate?"

He told her he would teach her karate if she would pay him by doing her homework. She wasn't too happy about that, but she agreed.

Mr. Miyagi had taught many people karate. His most recent pupil was a boy named Daniel La-Russo. Mr. Miyagi taught him karate techniques without him even knowing it! He showed him how to apply wax to a car, but he was really showing him how to block a punch by moving his hand in a circle.

Mr. Miyagi tried the same thing with Julie. It didn't work.

"Forget it. I'm not waxing anybody's car!"

"Wax car. Then we work on engine. This is fun," said Mr. Miyagi. Julie didn't agree. She wanted to go to the mall instead. The problem was that she didn't have any money. She ran up to her room to be alone.

6

A few minutes later, Mr. Miyagi knocked on her door and told her the neighbors needed a baby-sitter. Julie knew the neighbors. Their name was Wescott and their boys were wild. Julie figured she was tough, though, and she could definitely use the money.

The boys got right down to being wild. As soon as Mr. and Mrs. Wescott left, they started running around. Julie didn't know what to do. Then Mr. Miyagi showed up. Julie thought he was going to be a help, but instead, he was more like a Santa Claus. He had a whole basketful of toys — Nerf balls, flying saucers, and plastic baseball bats. The boys thought it was good news. Julie thought it was bad news. She told Mr. Miyagi so. He told her, "Sun is warm. Grass is green."

"What?" she asked.

"If you get angry today, breathe deep and repeat those words."

She wished he would make sense just once.

The minute Mr. Miyagi left the Wescotts' house, Julie was in trouble.

At first the problem was that she didn't know what the boys were up to. Then the problem was that she did!

She went upstairs to find them. Wesley threw a flying saucer at her. It hit her in the head. It hurt. It made her angry. She remembered Mr. Miyagi's suggestion.

"The sun is warm. The grass is green."

Next came a Nerf ball. Lawrence threw it from behind her. It just bounced off, but it annoyed her, too.

"The sun is warm. The grass is green."

Then Sean jumped out of a closet in front of her and swung a plastic bat at her shins. "Yeouch!" she screamed. Sean disappeared back into the closet.

"The sun is warm. The grass is green."

Julie turned around to see if she could find Lawrence and Wesley, but all three boys had disappeared! That made her even angrier.

"The sun is warm! The grass is green! You little creeps!"

She had no idea where the boys were. As long as they weren't attacking her, she didn't care, either.

She went back downstairs. On her way, she realized something. She was getting attacked by the boys because she was doing what they wanted — chasing after them. If she stopped doing that, she might not avoid attacks, but she thought she could avoid *successful* attacks.

"The sun is warm. The grass is green," she said. She started to think it might be true. Then, instead of thinking angry, vengeful thoughts, she began to think of sneaky ways to beat the boys at their own game. It was just a game.

She got a newspaper and a glass of milk. While she was pouring the milk, Wesley threw a Nerf ball at her. She caught it and stuck it in her pocket.

She walked to the living room. A flying saucer came whizzing toward her. She heard it before she saw it. She caught that, too. She carried it into the living room. She sat on the sofa in the living room. They wouldn't be able to sneak up on her there the way they could upstairs. She put the Nerf ball and the flying saucer on the seat next to her. She would wait there and collect all the boys' weapons, one by one. She smiled to herself. She began reading the paper.

Along came a Nerf ball. Julie blocked it with her arm. Then there was another flying saucer. She had to reach high to catch it, but she did. And then Lawrence came at her with the plastic bat. She blocked his attack with one hand and grabbed the bat from him with the other. He ran away. She put the bat on the sofa with the other toys.

The attacks continued all afternoon. Julie found that she couldn't keep the boys from attacking —

until she had all the toys — but, as she had hoped, she could keep the attacks from succeeding.

"The sun is warm. The grass is green." She said it a lot. She wasn't angry, either. She just wondered why it was that Mr. Miyagi had made it possible for the boys to torment her with the toys.

Just as Julie was finishing the newspaper, the doorbell rang. It was Mr. Miyagi.

"Mrs. Wescott call me. Say phone off the hook."

"It figures," said Julie.

"Parents come home in half an hour."

That was the best news Julie had had all day!

"What's wrong? Boys throw Nerf balls at you?"

"All afternoon," said Julie.

"Throw flying saucer? Try hit you with plastic bat?"

Julie was getting suspicious. How did Mr. Miyagi know what the boys would do?

"What's going on here?" she asked.

Mr. Miyagi raised his hand and moved it slowly toward her. "Defend yourself. Here come Nerf ball."

She put her hand up as if she were catching it.

He swung his other hand at her, at shoulder level, and swung it toward her. "Now flying saucer! Defend!"

Julie swatted at his hand just the way she had at the flying saucers.

Then Mr. Miyagi punched at her slowly with a

punch that came downward, aimed at her legs. She blocked the punch.

He did the same moves faster. Julie blocked his attacks, faster. Then they did it again, faster still.

"Nerf ball! Saucer! Bat!" he called out each time.

By then, Julie understood. She hadn't just been baby-sitting. She'd been learning karate! The boys had attacked, she had defended. And she'd done a good job of it, too!

Half an hour later, the Wescotts came home. Julie and Mr. Miyagi returned to Grandma's house.

"You planned that whole thing," Julie said.

"*Hai*. Baby-sitting good practice for karate student."

Julie thought that was exciting and she was sure she'd be even better once she got to real karate. "When do I learn how to break boards and stuff like that?" she asked.

"Why break boards? What they do to you? Learn how to conquer anger, Julie-san."

Julie thought breaking boards might be easier.

7

A few nights later, Julie had to go back to the school to feed Angel. This time, she wasn't going to let a passing policeman see her on the roof. She snuck in through the same window. She was being very quiet. She wasn't quiet enough, though, because the Alphas were right there, waiting for her!

Charlie, one of the Alphas, grabbed Julie's arms. He held her tightly.

"We knew somebody was trying to break into the school at night," said Ned. "Now we know who it is!"

Julie didn't like the look in his eye. She thought it would have been better if she'd been caught by policemen. She spun around and punched Charlie with her free arm until he let her go. Then she ran.

She ran down the hall. She ran into the staircase. She ran downstairs. She knew the school

28

very well and she knew that there was an exit through the kitchen.

The kitchen seemed odd at night, all dark and empty. There were rows of aluminum pots hanging up over the worktables. They sparkled in the dark room.

Julie was running so fast that she barely saw them. Then she saw the exit door and ran into that, hitting the bar as she ran. The door didn't open. It was locked.

She turned around to find another exit. Instead, she found Ned Randall.

"No way out, Julie," he said.

Julie was really scared. She didn't know what Ned was going to do to her, but she was sure she wasn't going to like it. She looked around, hoping to find some way to help herself.

She spotted some pots hanging over Ned's head. Ned grabbed for Julie. Julie grabbed for the pots. Before Ned knew what had happened, eight huge aluminum pots landed on him. While he climbed out from under them, Julie ran away.

She dashed through the lunchroom, along the hallway, up the stairs and out the front door of the school. Fresh air had never smelled so good in her whole life! Ned and the other Alphas were behind her, but she was fast and she was sure she'd find someone to help her. Then she saw a police car. She waved to it. The policemen stopped. Julie thought it was the most wonderful sight she'd ever seen — until she saw who got out of the police car: Col. Dugan!

Col. Dugan had believed Ned when Ned told him Julie had been smoking cigarettes. He would believe whatever Ned said this time. Julie knew she was in big trouble.

An hour later, she found out exactly how big the trouble was. Mr. Miyagi picked her up at the police station.

"What you doing at school, Julie-san?" he asked.

"I was trying to feed Angel."

"Would rather you *acted* like an angel," he said.

"Angel's a hawk, Mr. Miyagi. It's a long story."

"Miyagi ready to listen."

Julie had wanted to keep everything in her life a secret. Now, she knew she had to tell. Mr. Miyagi was being very nice and fair to her. She would do the same in return. She told him all about Angel. He listened and he didn't interrupt.

When she was done, he spoke.

"Not wrong to help hawk, Julie-san, but you should have told Miyagi."

Maybe she should have, but it was too late now.

"Dugan talked to the principal. They kicked me out of school for two weeks. Now I'll never catch up with my classes."

She was upset because she'd been working very hard to catch up and keep up, just so she could learn karate. Now it all seemed lost.

30

"Life can change," said Mr. Miyagi. "But you must keep trying. Tomorrow morning, we leave Boston for short time. Go to special place. Maybe you find new friends there."

Julie didn't think that would help. She also didn't think it would hurt. Nothing could be worse than the way things were now.

8

The next morning, Julie and Mr. Miyagi were up and ready to go very early. The sun wasn't even up yet. Mr. Miyagi wouldn't tell Julie where they were going. Julie didn't really care. She did care about Angel, though. She wouldn't leave until she knew that Angel would be fed.

Mr. Miyagi drove her to the train yard where Eric worked. He was there, standing on top of a train, watching the sunrise.

"Hey, Julie, what are you doing here?" Eric asked.

"Something happened at school and I got suspended. I'm going out of town for a couple of weeks. Think you could feed the hawk?"

"Sure. No problem."

"Give her raw meat every other day. And keep the water bottle filled."

"Don't worry. I'll remember. I'm going to miss you. Will you miss me?"

Julie hadn't thought about that. She didn't like to think about missing people. She liked to think she didn't miss anybody and nobody missed her. She liked to think she didn't need anybody enough to miss them. She wasn't sure about Eric, though.

"Maybe," she said.

That wasn't good enough for Eric. He definitely wanted to know that Julie would miss him and he made her promise. Finally, she promised. When she said it, she realized that it might even be true. That surprised her a little.

Mr. Miyagi and Julie said good-bye to Eric and got into their car. Julie still didn't know where they were going, but Mr. Miyagi said it was a long drive.

Julie went to sleep. She woke up when she felt the car turn into a driveway. She sat up and rubbed her eyes.

"Is this it? Is this place important?"

"Very important. Need gas," said Mr. Miyagi. Julie stopped rubbing her eyes. They were in an old run-down gas station! Mr. Miyagi gave her some money and asked her to pay for the gas and get him a chocolate bar. She went inside.

Inside was not a nice place. It was dark and dingy. Four men were there and they didn't look nice, either. They started teasing Julie. Julie didn't like it.

"Why don't you stay a while? Have a beer with us."

"Forget it," Julie said. She wanted to get out of there. She walked over to the door.

"Joey! Take it!" said one of the men. Joey was a big dog. He'd been sleeping, but the minute his owner, Ted, spoke to him, Joey jumped up. He stood in front of the door and he growled. Julie couldn't leave. The men laughed at her.

Then the door opened behind Joey. Mr. Miyagi came in. Joey growled at him. Mr. Miyagi crouched and spoke to him in Japanese. The next thing Julie knew, Mr. Miyagi was patting Joey and Joey's tail was wagging!

"Joey, you're supposed to bite him!" Ted said.

"Nice dog," said Mr. Miyagi.

Julie and Mr. Miyagi left as quickly as they could.

"How'd you do that, Mr. Miyagi? That dog was going to attack me."

"All things possible, if not afraid," he said.

"I wish I had your courage."

"Wish I had chocolate bar with almonds. Where is it?"

Julie didn't want to go back into the shop.

"I think we should just get the gas and . . ."

Before she could finish speaking, Ted and two of his friends came out of the shop. He was angrier than before.

"Hey! Look at my dog! What did you do to him? Get him, Joey! Get him!"

Joey just wagged his tail.

34

"Sometimes animals smarter than humans," said Mr. Miyagi. Julie knew which human Mr. Miyagi was thinking of when he said that, too.

Ted was angry. He grabbed Julie's arm to keep her from leaving. That made Mr. Miyagi angry.

"Let go of girl," he said.

"What are you going to do about it, old man? Going to fight?"

"Fighting not good," said Mr. Miyagi.

"I guess that means you're scared of me," said Ted. Then he let go of Julie and attacked Mr. Miyagi.

Mr. Miyagi caught Ted's arm and twisted it around behind him. One of Ted's friends decided to help Ted. It was a bad idea. When Ernie tried to kick Mr. Miyagi, Mr. Miyagi turned Ted so that Ernie actually kicked Ted! Then Mr. Miyagi jerked Ted's elbow so that it hit Ernie and knocked him out. When Roland, another one of the men, tried to help, Mr. Miyagi did the same thing. Julie *almost* felt sorry for Ted when his friend hit him with a tire iron. Then Mr. Miyagi used Ted like a battering ram and Roland ended up in the dirt, next to Ernie. In a second, Ted joined them.

"Fighting not good because people get hurt," said Mr. Miyagi.

Mr. Miyagi pumped the gas, and soon he and Julie were on the road.

"That was great, Mr. Miyagi!" said Julie.

"Not great. Unfortunate. Should find way not to fight."

"Come on! Aren't you glad you beat those bullies?"

"Not want to hurt anything. Want chocolate bar — with almonds."

9

Julie and Mr. Miyagi were staying in a monastery. It wasn't like any monastery Julie had ever heard of, either. It was a Buddhist monastery and there were only three monks there.

One of them was the abbot. He was older than the others and seemed to be someone Mr. Miyagi had known for a long time. Then there was a tall monk and a plump monk. Julie didn't know their names or anything about them. She just knew that they were staying there and it was strange.

For one thing, they'd had to wait for hours before the monks had opened the door for them. Mr. Miyagi said that it was a way of learning patience and Julie shouldn't expect to find a lost treasure easily. Julie didn't know what he was talking about. She didn't recall losing anything.

Another thing that was strange was her room. She had a small chamber and it didn't have any furniture in it. She slept on a cotton pad on the floor. It was called a futon. She was so tired that she slept very well. She woke up hungry. That was when she learned the next strange thing. They didn't serve breakfast in the monastery. There were only two meals and the first one was lunch.

Julie thought about whining and complaining and decided not to. She didn't know how to make her life better, but she knew that what she had been doing hadn't been working. She wanted to try to begin a new life. If she didn't try, she'd never know if she'd missed a chance. She had decided to try very hard to do whatever Mr. Miyagi asked. Anyone who could beat up bullies the way he had taken care of those three guys yesterday was someone worth listening to.

She followed Mr. Miyagi into a garden where he said they would work on her karate. On their way there, she saw the abbot. He had a little broom made of feathers and he was brushing the ground in front of him as he walked.

Julie thought he was some kind of neat freak.

"Broom not for dust. Broom for bugs," Mr. Miyagi said.

"What?"

"This monk take vow never to kill a living thing — not even an ant or a spider. When he's outside, he uses broom to push them away." Julie thought that was the strangest thing of all about the monastery!

Julie and Mr. Miyagi walked to a place he called

the "Zen garden." It had more rocks than plants. It was very plain, but somehow very beautiful. Mr. Miyagi explained that Zen was a kind of meditation. The idea of the garden was to be able to think and meditate there. They weren't going to meditate, though. They were going to have a karate lesson.

Mr. Miyagi told Julie to climb up on one of the rocks. He told her it was Japan. She looked at it and she could see what he meant. It did look a little bit like the islands that made up the country of Japan.

"All right. I'm on Japan. Think I could buy a TV set or something while I'm here?" she joked.

"No TV set. Fake front kick at opponent, then roll over, make round kick, then visit Okinawa."

"Okinawa?"

"Small island where Miyagi born," he said, pointing to another rock.

Julie understood. If the big rock was Japan, the little one was Okinawa. It was about eight feet away, across a lot of gravel that was the China Sea. Eight feet was a very big jump, especially if she had to kick, roll, and kick again as she went.

She tried. She landed on the ground, less than halfway to "Okinawa."

"That's impossible!" she said.

"Most things impossible — until we do them. Focus, Julie-san. Try again."

"Is there a trick to this?"

"Pray," said Mr. Miyagi.

There he went, once again saying things that didn't make any sense. Still, she wanted to be able to do it. She tried. It didn't work.

"Try again," he said.

She tried again. She tried a lot, but she never even got close.

"At this rate, I'm never going to make it to Okinawa. My technique is lousy."

"Technique will improve. Attitude more important."

"What's wrong with my attitude?"

"When little girl is growing up, adults say 'Be good. Wear pretty dress. Don't fight.' "

"And she gets scared?" Julie said.

"*Hai*. In dangerous situation, girl hesitate. Wait for permission."

"So when *is* it okay to use karate?" Julie asked.

"Respect self. Respect others. Answer will come."

After a while, Mr. Miyagi said it was time to try something else, and he took her into a barn on the monastery property. Julie didn't know what they were doing here.

"Must learn how to be alert, Julie-san. Always know where trouble is."

"All right, I'm alert," she said.

"Open eyes, Julie-san."

"My eyes *are* open. What am I supposed to . . ."

They weren't open enough, though, because

right then she was hit with a gunnysack full of hay, attached to a long rope. It knocked Julie onto the floor. She wasn't hurt, but she was a little confused. Then she saw that the plump monk was sitting on one of the rafters above and behind her in the barn. He'd knocked her down with the sack.

"Focus eyes," said Mr. Miyagi.

Julie wondered how she was expected to know when someone was going to knock her down from behind. What good would her eyes do in a situation like that?

10

Lunchtime was no better. The monks' idea of
lunch was some miso soup with a few vege-
tables in it. Julie was hungry enough to eat a
parsnip. She just pretended it was a double
cheeseburger with fries.

It took her only about two minutes to wolf it
down. She waited and watched while the others
ate slowly. Nobody talked. The monks seemed to
be meditating while they ate. So did Mr. Miyagi.

Julie looked around, trying to find something
interesting to look at. She saw a small bug. She
watched it crawl up the leg of the table and onto
the top of the table. Julie didn't like the idea of
sharing her lunch with a bug. She took off her
shoe and raised her arm high to smash the bug.
She smashed her shoe on the table, all right, but
not on the bug. Just before her shoe hit the table,
the tall monk reached out and swept the bug away
to safety.

Then all three monks stood up and walked away. They didn't seem at all happy.

"What's the problem?" Julie asked Mr. Miyagi.

"Julie-san tried to kill bug."

"What? You've never killed a bug before?"

"Monks believe all negative action causes pain and suffering. For this reason, nothing is killed within monastery walls."

"That's a stupid rule," said Julie.

"Stupid when gangs kill each other in street. Stupid when countries fight wars. Not stupid to respect all living things."

"I bet *you've* killed bugs," Julie said.

"Miyagi not live in monastery. But still respect life."

He left Julie alone then. For the next few days, she was as alone as she'd ever been in her whole life.

The monks wouldn't speak to her at all. Mr. Miyagi did speak to her, but not much. He worked with her on her karate and sometimes he ate with her. Most of the time, though, she was alone.

One day, after eating lunch alone, Julie was walking by the kitchen and heard loud laughing. She hadn't heard anybody laughing since they'd arrived at the monastery. She wondered who could be making such a sound. She looked in the kitchen. It was the monks and Mr. Miyagi! She'd thought there was some sort of monastery rule about laughter. She'd been wrong. It made her want to know more about the monks. As long as they were busy laughing, she'd do some exploring.

She found a closet that had some old suitcases in it. She looked in one and learned more than she would have believed. There was a picture of the abbot. He was in a U.S. Army World War II uniform. He was getting the Congressional Medal of Honor — just like the one her grandfather had!

Mr. Miyagi found her in the storage closet then.

"What you doing?" he asked.

"Look at this stuff, Mr. Miyagi."

"You should not be here," he said sternly.

"Okay, I'm sorry, but take a look!"

He looked. "Abbot was corporal in same regiment with Miyagi," he explained.

The Medal of Honor was the highest award the U.S. government could give a serviceman. People who got the medal killed a lot more than bugs!

"He killed hundreds of the enemy," said Mr. Miyagi. "More than anyone else. He was wounded in spirit. Changed."

"He seems okay nowadays," said Julie.

"He has found peace. Respect for life. It is great lesson for Miyagi."

A lesson for Mr. Miyagi? That didn't make sense to Julie. Then he said something that made even less sense.

"Should be lesson for *Julie-san*."

Julie was beginning to learn to listen to Mr. Miyagi. Sometimes the things he said meant more than one thing. When she thought about it, she thought she understood. Mr. Miyagi was telling her that *she* was wounded in spirit and had to find peace. Two weeks ago, she would have told him he was crazy and she would have run away from the house. Now, however, she couldn't run away because she wasn't at the house. She wasn't so sure he was crazy, either. She *was* wounded in spirit. She hadn't recovered from her parents' deaths. She was unhappy and angry. She wanted to find some inner peace for herself. That didn't mean she wouldn't ever kill a bug, but it might mean that she could understand someone who wouldn't kill a bug.

Julie put the suitcases and the pictures away. She had some thinking to do. She took a walk in a field. It was cold weather and the grass wasn't growing, but there were a few stalks there.

She lay down on the cool earth to think. While she was thinking, she saw a praying mantis. It was a long-legged, skinny green insect. She watched him. He climbed up a stalk of grass.

When he was climbing, his legs didn't move too much. When he saw a littler bug, it was a different story. All of a sudden, his legs straightened out, making him many times longer than he was when he was just sitting there. He jumped up, trapped his prey, and then folded back down again to enjoy dinner. Julie couldn't believe how far he had been able to reach.

Then she did some more thinking. She thought about the monks and she thought about herself. She wanted inner peace, just as the abbot had. In order to find peace, she was going to have to make it. In order to make peace with the monks, she'd have to show them that she did respect life. She had an idea.

Very carefully, she caught the praying mantis. She held it in her hands and carried it back to the monastery. She found a jar and poked holes in its top. She put the praying mantis inside and went to find the monks.

They were meditating. Their meditation hall was a big room. It had a statue of Buddha at one end of it. Buddha seemed to be meditating, too. Julie didn't like to interrupt, but she didn't want to wait.

She handed the jar to the tall monk because he was the one who had brushed the bug away from her shoe. He examined the jar, nodded, and passed it on to the plump monk. The plump monk looked, too. Then he handed it to the abbot. The abbot opened the jar and let the praying mantis out the window.

"Good," he said.

Julie knew she'd done the right thing and it felt very good.

11

After that, Julie began working even harder on her karate. She still couldn't get from "Japan" to "Okinawa," but she got very good at opening her eyes in the barn. She even learned to focus so well that she could "see" with a blindfold on! She could almost feel the gunnysack coming her way. She blocked and punched and felt very proud of herself — until two more gunnysacks came out of nowhere. Mr. Miyagi always seemed to be one step ahead of her! That made her want to work harder.

One night, she was practicing alone. She was performing a *kata*. That meant she was doing a series of moves — blocks, kicks, punches — almost like a dance. It was so much like a dance that she'd decided to do it to music. She was glad she'd brought her tape deck and some rock music with her. She plugged in the tape deck and started playing Prince's music.

She didn't even notice when the monks came into the room. When she saw them watching her, she was upset. She'd worked very hard to become friendly with them. Now, she thought she'd blown the whole thing!

"I'm sorry. Really sorry. I thought you guys were asleep," she said.

The monks walked toward her. She tried to unplug her tape deck, but tripped on some cassettes instead. The monks moved closer still. Then they started sort of swaying together. It looked very strange. It got stranger when they began walking around and swaying at the same time. Mr. Miyagi came into the room.

"What are they doing?" Julie asked.

"Nothing much. Just having fun."

"Fun? These guys are monks! They're not supposed to have fun."

"Never trust a man who can't dance," said Mr. Miyagi. Then he started dancing, too. Julie did the only logical thing. She joined in on the fun. She was really getting to like these guys.

The next day, Julie and Mr. Miyagi were back in the Zen garden.

"I can't do it. I've tried a thousand times," Julie said.

"Remember what I tell you?"

"Pray?"

"Like praying mantis."

Julie remembered. She remembered watching the praying mantis, too. He'd been sort of folded up and then he'd sprung at his prey. If Julie bent down on one knee, she'd be sort of folded up, too.

Julie tried it. She pushed herself up and off the rock by straightening her legs. She shot into the air. She faked a front kick, rolled over into a round kick and landed flat on her feet — on Okinawa!

She was very happy. "Do I get a belt or something?" she asked.

"Buy belt at mall," Mr. Miyagi said.

"I mean a *karate* belt. You know. Brown belt. Black belt, so everybody knows how good I am."

"You know that you're good. That most important thing," said Mr. Miyagi. Julie understood. Knowing she was good was a kind of inner peace.

12

The last night at the monastery was Julie's birthday. The monks gave Julie a birthday party and that was the strangest thing of all.

For one thing, Julie had never eaten birthday cake with chopsticks. She thought it tasted even better with chopsticks than with Grandma's silver forks.

For another thing, they told her for her birthday they would give her one wish and one gift. She thought about her wish and decided that the nicest thing they could do for her would be to come visit her and Mr. Miyagi at Grandma's house.

At first, the monks didn't know what to say to that. They hadn't left the monastery in a long time. They decided it was a good idea and promised they'd come. Then it was time for her gift.

The monks took Julie and Mr. Miyagi down a hallway and into the meditation hall.

"What's going on, Mr. Miyagi?" Julie asked.

"Your gift is demonstration of Zen archery. My friend has not used bow for twelve years. He just meditated about shooting. Very rare to see this."

It didn't seem too special to Julie, especially when she saw that he was only going to shoot one arrow.

"So where's the target?" Julie asked Mr. Miyagi.

"You're looking at it," he answered. He meant the monk was going to shoot at *him*. "Miyagi has received this honor."

Julie didn't think it was an honor. However, if she'd learned one thing in the last two weeks, it was to keep quiet and watch.

Mr. Miyagi went to one end of the hall. The abbot stood at the other with his arrow. When he was ready, he put the arrow in the bow. Then he pulled back the string and aimed. He was aiming right *at* Mr. Miyagi. Julie wanted to scream. Instead, she kept quiet and watched.

The abbot released the string. The arrow went right at Mr. Miyagi's head. He didn't move his head. He just moved his right hand and caught the arrow!

Julie gasped. The abbot walked over to Mr. Miyagi and bowed. Mr. Miyagi handed him the arrow. The abbot walked over to Julie and bowed. Then he offered her the arrow. She bowed to him and accepted it.

That was when she understood how precious her gift was. The abbot and Mr. Miyagi had demonstrated the power of focus, concentration, and attitude. It was everything Mr. Miyagi was trying to teach her about karate.

She knew then that she'd learned a lot in the past two weeks and it wasn't all just kicking and blocking. She'd learned about herself.

13

Two days later, Julie was back in school. Mr. Wilkes, the principal, met her on her way in.

"I'm sorry about what happened," she told him.

He was surprised and pleased. "It sounds like you've learned something in the last two weeks."

She had learned a lot. She wanted him to understand how she felt. She told him one of the things Mr. Miyagi had taught her. "Ambition without knowledge is like a boat on dry land."

"I don't quite understand," he said.

"The answer is not important if you ask the right question," she said. Then she went into the school. She knew Mr. Wilkes was even more confused now, and she thought that was just fine.

At lunch, she saw Eric for the first time.

"How's Angel?" she asked.

"She looks good," Eric said. "These days we're best friends."

Julie thought that was okay.

She thought Eric was a good friend to her, too.

Then he surprised her. First, he told her that he'd quit the Alpha Elite.

"How will you get into the Air Force Academy without Col. Dugan?" Julie asked.

"I don't need him. He's been giving orders for so long it's warped his brain."

Julie thought Eric was right and she was glad to know that was the way he felt. Then Eric surprised her again. He asked her to the Senior Prom. It was the biggest dance of the year. Julie hadn't even thought about going to it and she didn't know what to say to Eric.

"Yes. No. We'll talk about it later," she said. First, she wanted to go visit Angel on the roof.

But Angel wasn't there. The cage door was open and there was no sign of Angel!

"I don't know what happened. She was here yesterday when I fed her," said Eric.

"Angel's wing is still injured. She couldn't fly away," said Julie.

She looked around for an answer and then it appeared. It was Ned Randall.

"What's the matter, Julie? Lose your little birdie?"

"What did you do with it? I want to know!" Julie said. She was very angry. Ned seemed pleased about that.

"I forget. You know, a bird like that, one that can't fly, might end up in a Dumpster!"

That was enough to make Eric furious. He attacked Ned and knocked him down. He held him still long enough for Julie to find out what had happened. The Alphas had called animal control and they'd taken Angel away.

"The man came and put it in a cage," Ned said. "Bet he'll kill that bird — and stuff it."

Eric was going to punch Ned again, but Julie said he shouldn't bother. They had to go rescue Angel. That was more important than punching Ned. Eric agreed. He let Ned go. Ned was angry that Eric had pinned him. He didn't like to be showed up. Before he left, Ned spoke to Eric.

"I'm not done with you. Don't forget. One way or another, we're going to finish this thing."

Julie and Eric hardly noticed. They were much more concerned about the hawk.

Julie ran all the way home from school and got Mr. Miyagi to drive her over to the animal shelter. Angel was okay. Julie was very relieved.

She carried Angel back out to the car and waited for Mr. Miyagi to drive her to the school. Instead, he took a longer trip into the woods and up on a hill.

"Angel ready to fly," Mr. Miyagi said.

"That's impossible, Mr. Miyagi. She's got a broken wing."

"Angel's decision. Not yours, Julie-san," said Mr. Miyagi.

A few minutes later, Julie stood on the edge of the hill. Angel was on her hand. The bird didn't move.

"I told you. Her wing's broken. She can't fly."

"We shall see," said Mr. Miyagi.

Julie moved her arm upwards as if she were throwing the bird in the air. Angel took off. She flew about twenty feet up and then came right back again.

"I told you so."

"Again. Now let wind touch bird."

Julie didn't want to, but she knew that the bird had to be free when she was ready. Maybe the bird was ready. Maybe it was Julie who wasn't ready. She patted the bird. She tried again.

This time Angel flew higher and higher. She moved her wings until they rested on the wind and then she soared in a big circle. She came back above where Julie and Mr. Miyagi were standing. She flapped her wings once. It was sort of a salute. Then she took off.

Julie knew she could be sad, but she wasn't. She was just happy that Angel was free.

"I'm going to miss Angel," she said to Mr. Miyagi. "I used to talk to her a lot. I would tell her what was going on."

"Talk to Miyagi or friend Eric," Mr. Miyagi suggested.

"Things are kind of changing between Eric and

me," Julie said. "He invited me to the Senior Prom. I said I'd think it over."

"What is problem? Don't like boy?"

"Sure I like him. But it's a formal dance and I don't have a dress. Even if I did, I don't have any idea how to dance. What if they played a waltz or something?"

"All things possible," said Mr. Miyagi.

Maybe it was possible to feel a gunnysack coming from behind. Maybe it was possible to jump eight feet and deliver a block and a kick at the same time. Waltzing was something else.

14

The next day, when Julie came home from school, she was ready to practice her karate as usual. Mr. Miyagi was doing something unusual, though. He told her they would practice indoors. He'd moved all the furniture aside in the living room.

"In here," he said.

Julie put down her jacket and her books. She was ready to practice karate anytime, anyplace.

"You ready?"

"Okay," Julie said.

"Sweep left leg."

She did it.

"Head block, left arm. Front kick, right leg. Downward block, right fist. Repeat."

It was an odd set of motions, but she could do it. She did it again.

"Concentrate, focus. Move a little bit to right at end. Now turn."

Julie turned.

"Now slow down. Slower. Slower."

She slowed down.

"Keep going," said Mr. Miyagi.

She kept doing the motions. Then he stood up and walked over to Grandma's record player. He pushed a button and music began. It was a waltz.

Julie was beginning to get the idea that this wasn't a karate lesson. Mr. Miyagi walked over to her and began dancing with her.

"I can't believe it. I'm waltzing. Where did you learn how to do this?"

"In France, during war. Your grandfather and Miyagi in Paris together. He said, 'If you can fight, you can dance.' "

Julie liked that. When she studied karate, she was learning something Mr. Miyagi had taught her grandfather. Now she was learning to waltz — just as her grandfather had taught Mr. Miyagi!

She turned and twirled gracefully. She was having fun, but she still had a worry about the dance.

"I don't know what I'm going to wear to this thing."

"Have suggestion," said Mr. Miyagi. Then he stopped dancing and he gave her a box. She opened it. Inside was the most beautiful dress she'd ever seen. It was perfect. She loved it and she knew Eric would, too.

"It's too bad you never had a daughter, Mr. Miyagi. You would have been a good parent."

Mr. Miyagi bowed to Julie and asked her to dance some more. She was only too happy to do it.

They were on their third waltz when the doorbell rang. Julie opened the door. It was the monks. All of Julie's dreams were coming true on the same day!

15

The monks really liked visiting Grandma's house. Mr. Miyagi and Julie liked having them there. They were enjoying modern American life. Mr. Miyagi had promised to take them all bowling while Julie was at the prom. Julie thought that would be fun, but she was glad she was going to the dance with Eric.

She finished her makeup and her hair and then she put on the dress. She looked wonderful and she knew it. Eric would think so, too. That made Julie feel even better.

She heard the doorbell ring. A few minutes later, Mr. Miyagi came up to her room and knocked on the door.

"Julie-san! Friend Eric is here," he said through the door. She told him to come in. "Very beautiful!" he said.

"I wish my parents could see this."

"They be very proud. Very happy. Enjoy dance, Julie-san."

She said she would.

Eric looked good, too. He was wearing a tuxedo and he had a flower for her. Mr. Miyagi and the monks took some pictures of them and then said good-bye.

"Who were all those people?" Eric asked.

Julie couldn't think of an easy way to describe them. "Friends," she said.

"I like them," said Eric.

"I like them, too," said Julie.

A few minutes later, Mr. Miyagi and the monks were in a car, heading for a bowling alley.

"You sure you want to do this?" Mr. Miyagi asked.

"*Hai*," they all said at once.

It was Saturday night at the bowling alley and the place was packed. Some people were wearing league bowling shirts. Some were wearing blue jeans. A few were in sweat pants or slacks. Only three people were wearing traditional Buddhist monk robes of orange cotton. Everybody looked at them when they came in.

"Want lane. Shoes. Bowling balls," said Mr. Miyagi.

The manager's eyes popped out of his head, but he gave them what they wanted.

Their lane was next to a group of serious bowlers. There were four men. One of them, Larry, eyed the monks suspiciously. He almost growled when the plump monk put his ball on the return rack.

"Don't touch my ball," said Larry. "This ball cost serious money!"

The plump monk spoke to him politely in Japanese.

"Don't talk, either. Don't breathe. Don't move. I don't want any distractions."

"What is problem here?" Mr. Miyagi asked.

"Why are these guys bowling in their nightgowns?" Larry asked.

His friend Jack teased him. "I bet they bowl as well as you do," he said.

"No way," said Larry.

Mr. Miyagi had an idea. "Perhaps we could have bowling contest. Dollar a point?"

Larry looked at Mr. Miyagi. He looked at the monks. "Dollar a point? You bet!"

Mr. Miyagi asked the monks if they'd like to bowl with these men.

"*Hai!*" they answered. The game was on.

Over at the high school, there was another kind of challenge going on.

As soon as Julie and Eric walked in, Julie knew they weren't welcome. She saw two of the Alphas staring down at them from the balcony over the gym. They pointed and glared at Julie and Eric.

"I guess some people don't want us here," said Julie.

Eric shrugged. "Come on. Let's dance," he said.

They went onto the dance floor and began dancing. Julie thought it was more fun to dance with Eric than with Mr. Miyagi. She felt badly for Eric, though.

"I'm sorry," she said.

"Sorry for what?"

"For getting you in trouble with Ned and his friends."

"You're worth it," said Eric.

Julie hoped that was true. She had the feeling that the worst wasn't over yet.

16

Larry was strong. He hurled the bowling ball down the lane. It whizzed along the boards, aimed right between the number one and number three pins at the end of the lane. Ca-rash! It zoomed through the pins, knocking seven of them down.

He looked at the plump monk. His look was a challenge. The plump monk picked up his ball. He closed his eyes. He took in a deep breath of air. He let it out slowly. He held the ball with two hands. He stood still for a moment. His eyes stayed closed. Then he leaned forward and pushed the ball down the lane.

It rolled and it rolled. It went very slowly, but it never changed direction. It hit the pins perfectly and knocked every one of them down!

People standing around clapped. This was the fourth strike that one of the monks had thrown. They had drawn a crowd.

"Why do they keep their eyes closed?" Jack asked Mr. Miyagi.

"Zen bowling," he explained. "Just think of target. No need to see."

The tall monk stood up then. He did almost exactly what his friend had done, and the ball did the same thing, too. It was another strike!

Larry was ready to try for his spare. He was sure he could do it, but he was wrong. He hurled the ball down the lane. It knocked down two of the pins. One was still standing. He decided to watch the monks' technique more carefully.

This time, it was the abbot's turn. He took his ball and studied it. He held it with two hands and rolled it toward the pins. This time, the ball didn't go straight down the lane. It went into the gutter.

"Awwww," said the crowd. The abbot didn't move. The ball did, though. It practically jumped back out of the gutter, skittered down the alley, and hit the pins. All of them went down.

"Wow!" said the crowd.

Larry couldn't believe his eyes. He couldn't believe his wallet, either. He and his friends had lost to these monks! Larry paid up. The monks bowed respectfully.

Mr. Wilkes walked up to the microphone next to the band in the gym. He cleared his throat. Everybody stopped dancing to listen to him.

"We've had a tradition here where the students provide special entertainment at the Senior Prom. This year, Col. Dugan and the Alpha Elite have volunteered."

Julie didn't like the sound of this. She liked it even less when Col. Dugan practically grabbed the microphone from Mr. Wilkes.

"Don't expect to watch us march in formation or anything," he said. "We don't 'march' in the Alpha Elite. We learn strength and endurance. We destroy our fear."

That was a cue. Right then, two of the Alphas turned on big spotlights and pointed them at the ceiling. The gym was three stories high. There were beams up there, and three of the Alphas were standing on the highest beams.

As soon as the lights reached them, all three boys jumped!

Strength and endurance was one thing. Suicide was another. The crowd screamed.

Then Julie saw that they were actually attached to bungee cords on each ankle. The boys stopped falling downward and bounced back up. It was weird, but it was a relief to know they were all okay.

All except for one of them. His name was TJ. The binding broke on one of his bungee cords, and

TJ started bouncing around wildly. He swung almost to the floor. Then he swept back upward. Then he came down again and slammed into the refreshment table. He was hurt.

Eric ran over to him. He helped him out of the binding and lowered him to the floor. Some of the other boys helped, too.

"I hurt my arm. It hurts badly!" said TJ. Eric took off his necktie and gave it to TJ to use as a sling.

Then Ned arrived. He didn't like the idea that Eric was rescuing one of the Alphas.

"Let him go!"

"Great idea, Ned. I think you just broke your friend's arm."

"At least he was brave enough to try it," said Ned.

"Not brave. Just stupid," said Eric.

That made Ned very angry. Before he could do anything about it, though, Mr. Wilkes arrived. He was the one who'd thought the Alphas would march. He was upset about what they had done. He was more upset about the fact that TJ had gotten hurt.

"This whole jump thing was totally unauthorized!" he said.

"Dugan's crazy," said Eric. "You know that, don't you? He's going to kill somebody one of these days!"

Mr. Wilkes seemed to realize that Eric was right. That was all Eric could expect. Eric turned to Julie.

"Come on. Let's get out of here," he said.

Julie was ready to go. She wanted to spend more time with Eric, but she didn't want to be anywhere near the school or the Alphas or Col. Dugan. Together, they went to Eric's car. Eric said he'd drive her home, very slowly. Neither of them wanted the evening to end. They particularly didn't want it to end that way.

At the bowling alley, the evening was ending on a much better note. Larry was wearing a blindfold.

"This is not going to work," he said. "I haven't had a strike all night."

The plump monk didn't understand a word he was saying, so he didn't pay any attention. He just led Larry to the head of the lane and handed him a bowling ball.

Mr. Miyagi and Jack were watching.

"Tell friend to have faith," said Mr. Miyagi.

"Come on, Larry! Zen bowling! You can do it, man!" said Jack.

Larry took a deep breath. He let it out slowly. He swung the ball gently back. Then he brought his hand forward and released. As soon as the ball hit wood, Larry pulled off his blindfold.

The ball went straight down the alley. It met with the pins. It knocked them down. All of them.

The crowd cheered. Larry jumped up and down. Then he hugged the plump monk.

"Hey! Can I buy you guys a beer?" said Larry.

"*Hai*," said the monks.

"Time to go home," said Mr. Miyagi.

17

Eric and Julie were sitting in Eric's car. They were in front of Julie's house. Inside, they could see Mr. Miyagi and the monks swinging their arms as if they were still bowling. Julie wondered how the evening had gone for them. That could wait, though. For now, she was happy just being with Eric.

"I'm sorry we couldn't stay at the dance," he said.

"None of this would have happened if you hadn't been with me," said Julie.

"I'm glad that it happened. It was time for me to break away from Col. Dugan and live my own life."

"Sometimes that's difficult," said Julie.

"It's easy when I'm with you," Eric said.

Suddenly, Eric's windshield was shattered and Ned Randall's face appeared, glaring at Eric and Julie.

"Meet you at the quarry, McGowen! If you're brave enough to go!" With that, Ned ran to the rear of the car and smashed the back window as well.

Then he jumped into his own car and drove away.

Julie and Eric jumped out of the car. She was almost too stunned to speak.

"Let's call the police," she said, finally.

"What for? They'll just lie about what happened."

Julie knew he was right.

"What are you going to do?" she asked.

"Drive to the quarry," he said.

"I'm going with you."

"I've got to do this myself. I've got to end it, once and for all," said Eric. He got back into his car, started the engine, and drove off before Julie could say anything.

Mr. Miyagi and the monks came out of the house. Julie told them what happened.

"Where is quarry?" asked Mr. Miyagi.

"Five or six miles out of town," said Julie.

"Wrong for Eric to go alone. Angry man dangerous to himself."

For once, Julie understood just exactly what Mr. Miyagi was saying. There wasn't a minute to waste.

"I'll change into my jeans. You start the car," she said.

Less than two minutes later, Julie and Mr. Miyagi were on their way to the quarry. Eric had been so angry that he hadn't seen what was really happening. There was no way Ned would challenge him to a fair fight. Julie knew that all the Alphas would be at the quarry. Eric didn't have a chance by himself.

As soon as Mr. Miyagi drew up to the parking area, she knew she'd been right. Ned's car was there, but there were five or six other cars there as well. She even saw Col. Dugan's car!

She and Mr. Miyagi jumped out of the car and went to where they could hear loud shouts. The shouts were for victory. Eric had been defeated. One by one, the Alphas had taken him on. He was lying in the dirt. He was bleeding.

"Eric!" Julie yelled. She ran to him.

"Get out of here. They'll hurt you," he said.

"I call police," Mr. Miyagi said to Col. Dugan.

"We'll just explain about the little accident this guy had," said Col. Dugan.

"No accident when six fight against one," said Mr. Miyagi.

"That doesn't make any difference," Col. Dugan said. "Ned here could have destroyed him with his hands behind his back."

Julie looked at Eric. She looked at Mr. Miyagi. She looked at Ned. She knew what she wanted to do. She knew what she had to do. Eric had been fighting with Ned because of her. It was really

73

her fight with Ned. She was the one who had to finish it, not Eric.

"Let me fight him," she said to Mr. Miyagi.

Ned thought that was a great idea. "That's okay with me, baby!" he sneered.

"Good idea, Ned," said Col. Dugan.

Julie helped Eric to a rock where he could sit safely. Then she consulted with Mr. Miyagi.

"He's stronger than me," she said.

"Never forget, Julie-san. Real strength comes from heart."

Julie knew that was true.

Ned took his first swing. Julie ducked underneath it, pretending to have been knocked down. As she fell to the ground, she kicked Ned's legs. He landed flat on the ground. She jumped up and continued the attack.

Ned was stunned, but he was good. He stood up again.

"You think I'd ever let a girl beat me, huh?" he asked.

Julie didn't think it mattered that she was a girl. She thought it mattered that she was better at fighting than he was. In the split second that she told herself that, she lost ground. Ned attacked her and she fell on the ground.

"Focus, Julie. *Focus!*" said Mr. Miyagi.

Julie focused. She pulled herself to her knees. Ned thought she was on her knees because she was wounded and weak. That was his mistake. She was there because she was praying!

In a split second, she propelled herself upward, just like the praying mantis. She faked a kick to the right and delivered a roundhouse kick with her left foot. It caught Ned totally by surprise and knocked him off his feet into the dirt. He'd lost and he knew it. So did almost everybody else.

"All over now, Julie-san. We go," said Mr. Miyagi.

"What are you talking about?" Col. Dugan demanded. "A war's not over because of one battle. Somebody else fight her! Let's go, men!"

One of the boys stood up to face Julie. Ned stopped him. "Forget it. Leave her alone," he said.

"That's an order!" said Col. Dugan.

It was an order nobody followed.

Mr. Miyagi and Julie began to walk toward the car. None of the Alphas moved to stop them.

That made Col. Dugan very angry. He began punching a few of the boys. He wanted them to be angry enough to fight Julie. They weren't angry at Julie. They were angry at Col. Dugan.

"This war isn't over, old man," Col. Dugan sneered.

"Then *we* will finish it. You and me," said Mr. Miyagi.

"Yeah. Let's do it," said Col. Dugan.

Col. Dugan didn't know what he was getting into. He didn't know that Mr. Miyagi had taught Julie everything she knew. He didn't know that there were three men at a gas station who wished they'd never met him.

"When a man fight with hate and anger, he become animal," said Mr. Miyagi.

Col. Dugan punched at him wildly.

"First he's a monkey, swinging his arms."

A swift kick made the colonel double over. He charged at Mr. Miyagi.

"Like a bull he rush forward," said Mr. Miyagi. He countered Col. Dugan's attack with some fast punches. The colonel ended up on the ground.

"Finally, he become dog on four legs," said Mr. Miyagi.

One more punch and the colonel was lying on the ground.

"And end up like a worm in mud."

That was a good way to describe him. Col. Dugan had really lost this time. Everybody knew it.

"How'd you do that?" Ned asked. "Col. Dugan's *got* to be stronger than you."

"More important is what you believe. True strength comes from what is in your heart," said Mr. Miyagi.

That made Ned think a little bit. "I'm kind of confused right now. I'm not sure what I believe."

Mr. Miyagi nodded. "Good first step," he said. "Now take another."

Mr. Miyagi turned to Eric and Julie. The three of them walked toward the car. It was time to go home. The battle was over, the war was won. There was no need to stay. Whatever the Alphas did, they wouldn't bother Julie and Eric anymore. Julie had the feeling they wouldn't bother anybody anymore.

Once again, Mr. Miyagi was right.